J. C. Ryle's Children's Stories

Children's Stories

J.C. Ryle

Published by Christian
Focus Publications

© 2001 Christian Focus Publications
ISBN 1-85792-639-0

Published by
Christian Focus Publications Ltd,
Geanies House, Fearn, Tain, Ross-shire
IV20 1TW, Scotland, Great Britain
www.christianfocus.com
email: info@christianfocus.com

Cover design by Catherine Mackenzie.

Printed and bound by

JOHN CHARLES RYLE
(1816 – 1900)
Bishop of Liverpool, 1880 - 1900

John Charles Ryle was born at Macclesfield in the north of England in 1816. The son of a wealthy banker, he was educated at Eton and Oxford University and was destined for a career in politics. Ryle was also a fine athlete who rowed and played cricket for Oxford and went on to gain a first class degree in Modern Greats.

As a result of hearing Ephesians chapter 2 read at church, Ryle became a Christian at the age of twenty-two and was ordained four years later, in 1842. He then ministered in several country churches before being appointed as the first Bishop of Liverpool in 1880.

Ryle was a well-known writer of many tracts and books as well as a faithful pastor. His commanding presence and fearless advocacy of his principles were combined with a kind and understanding attitude in his personal relationships, which particularly endeared him to children.

CONTENTS

The Two Bears

"He went up from thence unto Bethel : and as he was going up by the way there came forth little children out of the city, and mocked him, and said unto him, Go up, thou bald head, go up, thou bald head.

"And he turned back, and looked on them, and cursed them in the name of the Lord. And there came forth two she bears out of the wood, and tare forty and two children of them."

2 KINGS 2. 23-24.

Dear Children,

Did you ever see a bear? Perhaps not. There are no wild bears in this country now. There are some kept at circuses and zoos, but there are none loose in the woods and fields. So perhaps you have never seen a bear.

A bear is a large, shaggy, wild animal, with great teeth and claws, and is very strong. It will kill sheep, and lambs, and calves, and goats, and eat them. It will sometimes even attack men, women or children. She-bears that have little cubs are particularly fierce and cruel. How thankful we ought to be, that we can walk about in England without fear of being caught by a bear!

Now I am going to tell you a story about a good man, two bears and some children. It is a story out of the Bible, and so you may be sure that it is all true. Stories in other books are often only "make-believe," and tell us things that never really happened. Stories out of the Bible, you must always remember are true, every word. Never forget that!

Once upon a time, many hundreds of years ago, there lived a good man whose name was Elisha. He was at first servant to a famous prophet of God named Elijah. After Elijah was taken up to heaven in a chariot of fire, Elisha was appointed to be prophet in his place. From that time to his death he was a very great and a very useful man. He did many miracles. He used to go up and down the land of Israel, teaching people how to serve God, and reproving sinners. In some places he kept up schools, called "schools of the prophets." In this way he became famous all over the country. All people knew Elisha, and all good people loved him.

One day, not long after Elijah had been taken up to heaven, Elisha went to a place called Bethel, where there was a school. I dare say he went to see how the school was getting on, and whether it was doing any good. All schools need looking after and examining ; and it does them good to be examined. It is only bad boys and girls who dislike being asked what they have learned.

Now as this good old man Elisha got near Bethel, a very sad thing happened. A great number of little children came out of the town, and behaved extremely badly. They began to mock Elisha, and called him names. Instead of respecting him, and bowing to him, like good children, they made fun of him, and said silly things. "Go up, thou bald head," they cried, "go up, thou bald head." They called him "bald head," I have no doubt, because the good prophet was bald with age, and had no hairs on his head. They said, "Go up," I suspect, because his master Elijah had lately gone up to heaven, as everybody knew. And they meant that Elisha had better go away after his master, and not trouble them any more with his teaching. It was as much as saying, "Be off and begone ! It is high time for you to go up, as well as your master."

Just think for a moment how wicked these children were! They lived in a town where they might have learned better things. There was a school of prophets at Bethel. But I am afraid they had not used their opportunities, and had loved play better than lessons. They had no business to mock Elisha, and treat him so badly. He had done them no harm, and had never been unkind to them. He was a good man, and one who was their best friend.

Above all, they ought not to have said, "Go up, and get away." They ought rather to have said, "Stay with us, and teach us the way to heaven." Truly it is sad to see to what lengths of wickedness even little children may go. It is sad to see how corrupt boys and girls can become, and what naughty things they will say, even when they should know better!

But what did Elisha do when these children behaved so badly? We are told that he "turned back and looked on them" with sorrow and displeasure. They had probably often done the same thing before. It had become a habit with them which could not be cured. The time had come when they must be punished.

We are then told that "he cursed them in the name of the Lord." That does not mean, you may be sure, that Elisha flew into a passion, and swore at the children as some bad old men might have done. He was not the man to do that! It only means that he solemnly pronounced God's anger and displeasure against them. He gravely told them, "in the name of the Lord," that God would certainly punish them, and that it was his duty as God's servant to say so. No, indeed! Elisha did not speak in passion or ill-temper just as a judge is not angry with the prisoner when he sentences him to be put in prison. When Elisha pronounced God's curse on these wicked children, he did it as God's appointed servant, firmly and faithfully, but in sorrow. God told him, no doubt, what to do, and like an obedient servant, he did it.

And what happened as soon as Elisha had spoken? At once there came out of a wood close by, two she-bears, which rushed upon these wicked children, tearing and killing all they caught.

Think what an awful shock that must have been! How dreadfully frightened these children must have felt! How sorry and ashamed of themselves they must have felt! But with many it was too late. Before they could get within the walls of Bethel the bears had caught and killed no less than forty-two little children. Forty two little boys and girls that night never came home to Bethel alive. Forty two little funerals took place next day! Many children, I hope, got home safe and were not hurt. But I am sure they would never forget what they had seen. They would remember the two bears as long as they lived.

Now, dear children, this is a sad story. But it is a very useful and instructive one. Like everything else in the Bible, it was written for your good. It teaches lessons which boys and girls ought never to forget. Let me tell you what those lessons are:-

(1) Learn, for one thing, that God *takes notice of what children do*.

He took notice of the "little children" at Bethel, and punished them for their wickedness. Remember, I beg of you, that God has not changed. He is still the same. He is every day taking notice of you.

I believe some people think that it

does not matter how children behave, because God only notices grown-up men and women. This is a very great mistake. The eyes of God are upon boys and girls, and He marks all they do. When they do right He is pleased, and when they do wrong He is displeased. Dear children, never forget this.

Let no one make you think that you are too young to serve God, and that you may safely wait till you are men and women. This is not true. It is never too soon to serve God. As soon as you know right from wrong, you are old enough to begin taking the right way. As soon as you are old enough to be punished for doing wrong, you are old enough to give your heart to God, and to follow Christ. The child that is old enough to be chastised for swearing and telling lies, is not too young to be taught to pray and read the Bible. The child that is big enough to displease God, is also big enough to please Him. The child that is old enough to be tempted by the devil, is not too young to have the grace of the Holy Spirit in his heart.

Children, however little and young you are, God is always noticing you. He notices how you behave at home, how you behave at school, and how you behave at play. He notices whether you say your prayers or not, and how you say them. He notices whether you mind what your mother tells you, and how you behave when out of your mother's sight. He notices whether you are greedy, selfish, cross, or tell lies, or take what is not your own. In short, there is nothing about children that God does not notice.

I read in the Bible, that when little Ishmael was almost dead with thirst in the wilderness, "God heard the voice of the lad." (Gen. 21. 17) Remember that, He listened to the child's prayer. I read, that when Samuel was only a little boy, God spoke to him. (I Sam. 3. 10) I read that when Abijah, the child of Jeroboam, was sick and dying, God said by the mouth of His prophet, "in him there is found some good thing toward the Lord God of Israel." (I Kings 14. 13) Children, these things were written for your learning.

Now I will give you a piece of advice. Say to yourselves every morning when you get up, "God sees me. Let me live as in God's sight." God is always looking at what you do, and hearing what you say. All is put down in His great books, and all must be reckoned for at the last day. It is written in the Bible, "Even a child is known by his doings." (Prov. 20. 11)

(2) Learn, for another thing, that it is *very wrong to mock good people, and despise their faith.*

The little children of Bethel mocked at Elisha, and called him "bald-head." Because of this they were terribly punished.

As long as you live, make it a rule never to mock a Christian or their faith.

This is one of the wickedest things you can do. It is pleasant to see boys and girls merry and happy. Youth is the time for laughter. But take care never to mock anyone belonging to God.

Some boys and girls, I am sorry to say, are very thoughtless about this. They think it clever to make fun of those who read their Bibles, and say their prayers, and keep the Sunday properly, and listen to what is said at church. They laugh at other boys and girls who listen to what their mothers say. They try to lead them astray. Some are so wicked, that when they see other children trying to do what pleases God, they will point their fingers at them, and shout out, "There goes a little *saint*."

Now all this is very wrong, and offends God exceedingly. There sits One in heaven who sees these wicked children, and when He sees them he is greatly displeased. We cannot wonder if such children end up in trouble, or turn out badly. All who despise God's people, despise God Himself. It is written, "Them that honour Me I will honour, and they that despise Me shall be lightly esteemed." (I Sam. 2. 30)

I read in the Bible that Ishmael was turned out of Abraham's house because he mocked his little brother Isaac.

St. Paul tells us about this, that "he persecuted him." (Gen. 21. 9 ; Gal. 4. 22-23 and 29) At the time when Ishmael did this he was only a boy. But, boy as he was, he was old enough to offend God by mocking, and to bring himself and his mother into great trouble.

Dear children, some of you perhaps have good fathers and mothers, who tell you to read your Bibles and say your prayers. I hope that you never laugh at them behind their backs, and mock at what they tell you about Jesus. Be sure, if you do this, that you commit a great sin. It is written, "The eye that mocketh at his father, and despiseth to obey his mother, the ravens of the valley shall pick it out, and the young eagles shall eat it." (Prov. 30. 17)

(3) Learn, in the last place, that *sin is sure to bring sorrow at last*.

Sin brought wounds and death on the children of Bethel. It brought weeping and crying to the homes of their parents. If these wicked boys and girls had not displeased God, they would not have been torn apart by the bears. Dear children, as long as you live, you will always see the same thing. Those who will have their own way and run into sin, are sure, sooner or later, to find themselves in trouble. This trouble may not come at once. It may even be kept off for many years. But sooner or later it is sure to come. There is a dreadful hell at last, and those who still go on sowing sin, are sure at last to reap sorrow.

Adam and Eve would eat the forbidden fruit in Eden, and what was the consequence? Sorrow. They were cast out of the garden with shame.

The people before the flood ate, and drank despising Noah's advice about the flood. And what was the consequence? Sorrow. The flood came, and they were all drowned.

The people of Sodom and Gomorrah would go on sinning in spite of Lot's warnings. And what was the consequence? Sorrow. The fire fell from heaven, and they were all burned.

Esau wanted to have the soup, and despised his birthright. And what was the consequence? Sorrow. He sought it afterwards too late, with many tears.

The children of Israel would not obey God's command, and go up into the land of Canaan, when He commanded them. And what was the consequence? Sorrow. They wandered forty years in the wilderness.

Achan, when Jericho was taken, would not obey the command of Joshua, but took money, and hid it under his tent. And what was the consequence? Sorrow. He was found out, and publicly stoned.

Judas Iscariot, one of the twelve Apostles, would not give his whole heart to Christ, but coveted money, and betrayed his Master. And what was the consequence? Sorrow. The money did him no good, and did not make him happy, and he hanged himself.

Ananias and Sapphira told a great lie to Peter and the Apostles, in order to be thought good, and yet keep hold of their riches at the same time. And what was the consequence? Sorrow. They were both struck dead in one day.

Dear children, remember these things to the end of your lives. The wages of sin is death. The fruit of sin at last is trouble. Those who tell lies, or steal, or break any commandments of God, may not suffer for it at first. But their sin will find them out. Sooner or later, in this world or the next, those that sow sin, like the children of Bethel, are sure to reap sorrow. And now I will finish all I have been saying with three parting pieces of advice. Consider them well, and lay them to heart.

(a) The way to be happy is to be really good in the sight of God. If you go your own way, and follow sin, you are sure to have trouble and sorrow.

(b) If you want to be really good, ask the Lord Jesus Christ to make you good, and to put His Spirit into your hearts. You cannot make yourselves good, I know. Your hearts are too weak, and the world and the devil are too strong. But Jesus Christ can make you good, and is ready and willing to do so. He can give you new hearts, and power to overcome sin.

Then take Jesus Christ for your Shepherd and Friend. Cast your souls upon Him. Jesus, who died on the cross to save us, has a special care for little children. He says:

"I love them that love Me, and those that seek Me early shall find Me."

"Suffer the little children to come

unto Me, and forbid them not, for of such is the kingdom of God." (Prov. 8.17; Mark 10.14)

(c) If you want to be kept from the evil that is in the world, remember daily that God sees you , and live as in God's sight. Never mock at good people, or make fun of their faith. Love those most who love God most, and choose for friends those who are God's friends. Hate sin of all sorts. When sinners entice you, do not consent. Turn away from that which is evil. Hold on to that which is good.

Dear children, if you live in this way, God will bless you, and you will find at last that you have "chosen the good part which cannot be taken from you." (Luke 10. 42)

Remember these things, and you will have learned something from the *"Two Bears."*

Children Walking in Truth.

"I rejoiced greatly that I found of thy children walking in truth."

2 JOHN 4.

Beloved Children,

The book from which my text is taken, is the shortest in the Bible. Look at it, when you go home, and you will find it so. It has only thirteen verses. But, short as it is, it is full of important things, and I think the verse I have just read is one of them.

The book is an Epistle, or Letter, written by the Apostle John. He wrote it to a good Christian lady, whom he knew. This lady had children, and some of them were the children spoken of in the text.

It seems that John found some of this good lady's children at a place where he happened to go ; and you see how well he found them behaving. He was able to write a good report of them to their mother, which we see in our text : "I rejoiced greatly that I found of thy children walking in truth."

Now, dear children, there are only two things I want to tell you about out of this text. Some of you perhaps are thinking this very minute, "What does walking in truth mean ?" Others perhaps are thinking, "Why did John rejoice so greatly ?" I shall try to answer these two questions.

(1) Firstly, I shall try to show you *when can it be said that children walk in truth ?*

(2) Secondly, I shall try to show you *what were the reasons that made the Apostle John rejoice so greatly?*

Dear children, let me ask you all one favour, let me ask you all to try to *listen.* I shall not keep you long. Come then, and listen to what I have to tell you. May the Holy Spirit open all your hearts, and bless what I say.

(1) I told you I would first try to show you this, *when can it be said that children walk in truth?* Let me set about it at once.

What does "*walking*" mean here? You must not think it means walking on our feet, as you have walked in here tonight. It means rather our way of behaving ourselves - our way of living and going on. And shall I tell you why the Bible calls this *"walking?"* It calls it so, because a man's life is just like a journey. From the time of our birth to the time of our death, we are always travelling and moving on. Life is a journey from the cradle to the grave, and a person's manner of living is, on that account, often called his *"walk."*

But what does *"walking in truth"* mean? It means walking in the ways of true faith in Christ, and not in the bad ways of this evil world. The world, I am sorry to tell you, is full of false notions and untruths, and specially full of untruths about Christianity. They all come from our great enemy, the devil.

The devil deceived Adam and Eve in Eden, and made them sin, by telling them a lie. He told them they would not die if they ate the forbidden fruit, and that was untrue. And the devil is always at the same work now. He is always trying to make men, and women, and children have false notions about God and about faith in Jesus. He persuades them to believe that what is really evil is good, and what is really good is evil - that God's service is not pleasant - and that sin will not harm them. And, I'm sad to say, vast numbers of people are deceived by him, and believe these untruths.

But those persons who walk in truth are very different. They pay no attention to the false notions there are in the world about Jesus and about Christianity. They follow the true way which God shows us in the Bible. Whatever others may do, their chief desire is to please God, and be His true servants. Now this was the character of the children spoken of in the text - John writes home to their mother and says, "I found them walking in truth."

Dear children, would you like to know whether you are walking in truth yourselves? Would you like to know how you can find out? Listen, every one of you, while I try to set these marks before you in order. Let every boy and girl come and hear what I am going to say.

(a) I tell you, then, for one thing, that children who walk in truth, *know the truth about sin.*

What is sin? To break any command of God is sin. To do anything that God says ought not to be done is sin. God is very holy, and very pure ; and every sin that is sinned displeases Him exceedingly. But, in spite of all this, most people in the world, both old and young, think very little about sin. Some try to make out they are not great sinners, and do not often break God's commandments. Others say that sin is not so terrible a thing after all, and that God is not so strict as people say He is. These are two great and dangerous mistakes.

Children who walk in truth think very differently. They have no such proud and high feelings. They feel themselves full of sin, and it grieves and humbles them. They believe that sin is the abominable thing which God hates. They look upon sin as their greatest enemy and plague. They hate it more than anything on earth. There is nothing they so heartily desire to be free from as sin.

Dear children, there is the first mark of walking in truth. Look at it. Think of it. *Do you hate sin ?*

(b) I tell you, for another thing, that children who walk in truth *love the true Saviour of sinners, and follow Him.*

There are few men and women who do not feel they need in some way to be saved. They feel that after death comes the judgment and they would like to be saved.

But alas, few of them will see that the Bible says there is only one Saviour, even Jesus Christ ; and few go to Jesus Christ and ask Him to save them. They trust rather in their own prayers, or their own repentance, or their own church-going, or their own goodness - or something of that kind. But these things, although useful in their place, cannot save one soul from hell. These are false ways of salvation. They cannot put away sin. They are not Christ.

Nothing can save you or me but Jesus Christ, who died for sinners on the cross. Those only who trust entirely in Him have their sins forgiven, and will go to heaven. These alone will find they have an Almighty Friend on the day of judgment. This is the true way to be saved.

Children who walk in truth have learned all this, and if you ask them what they put their trust in, they will answer, *"Nothing but Christ."* They remember His gracious words: "Suffer the little children to come unto Me, and forbid them not." They try to follow Jesus, as the lambs follow the good shepherd. And they loved Him, because they read in the Bible that He loved them, and gave Himself for them.

Little children, there is the second mark of walking in truth. Look at it. Think of it. *Do you love Christ?*

(c) I tell you, for a third thing, that children who walk in truth *serve God with a true heart.*

I dare say you know it is very possible to serve God with outward service only. Many do so. They will put on a solemn face, and pretend to be serious, while they do not feel it. They will say beautiful prayers with their lips, and yet not mean what they say. They will sit in their places at church every Sunday, and yet be thinking of other things all the time - and such service is outward service, and very wrong.

Bad children, I am sorry to say, are often guilty of this sin. They will say their prayers regularly, when their parents make them - but not otherwise. They will seem to listen in church when the minister's eye is upon them - but not at other times. Their *hearts* are far away.

Children who walk in truth are not so. They have another spirit in them. Their desire is to be honest in all they do with God, and to worship Him in spirit and in truth. When they pray, they try to be in earnest, and mean all the words they say. When they go to church they try to be really attentive, and to give their minds to what they hear. And it is one of their main concerns - that they cannot serve God more wholeheartedly than they do already.

Little children, there is the third mark of walking in truth. Look at it. Think of it. *Is your heart false or true?*

(d) I tell you, for a last thing, that children who walk in truth, *really try to do things right and true in the sight of God.*

God has told us very clearly what He thinks right. Nobody who reads the Bible with an honest heart can mistake this. But it is sad to see how few men and women care for pleasing God. Many break His commandments continually, and seem to think nothing of it. Some will tell lies, and swear, and quarrel, and cheat, and steal. Others use bad words, break the Sabbath, never pray to God at all, never read their Bibles. Others are unkind to their relations, or lazy, or greedy, or bad-tempered, or selfish. And all these things, whatever people may choose to think, are very wicked and displeasing to the holy God.

Children who walk in truth are always trying to keep clear of bad ways. They take no pleasure in sinful things of any kind, and they dislike the company of those who do them. Their great wish is to be like Jesus - holy, harmless, and separate from sinners. They try to be kind, gentle, obliging, obedient, honest, truthful, and good in all their ways. It upsets them they are not more holy than they are.

There is the last mark I shall give you of walking in truth. Look at it. Think of it. *Are your actions right or wrong?*

Children, you have now heard some marks of walking in truth. I have tried to set them plainly before you. I hope you have understood them.

- *Knowing the truth about sin.*
- *Loving the true Saviour, Jesus Christ.*
- *Serving God with a true heart.*
- *Doing the things that are true and right in the sight of God.*

There they are, all four together. Think about them and ask yourself this question - "What am I doing at this very time : am I walking in truth ?"

I'm sure that many boys and girls here know well what answer they should give. And God knows too, for He sees your hearts as plainly as I see your faces this minute. Children, the all-seeing God sends you a question this night by my mouth : He says, *Are you walking in truth?*

Why shouldn't you? Thousands of dear children have walked in truth already, and found it pleasant. The way is trodden by many little feet before your own. Thousands of boys and girls are walking in truth at this moment, and there is yet room. Dear children, think this night, *"Why shouldn't you?"* (2) And now I will go on to the second thing I promised to speak of.

I said I would try to show you some of the *reasons why John rejoiced to find this lady's children walking in truth.* Let me see about it. The text says, "I rejoiced greatly." Now why did he rejoice? There must have been some good reasons. John was not a man to rejoice without cause. Listen, dear children, and you shall hear what those reasons were.

(a) For one thing, John rejoiced *because he was a good man himself.*

All good people like to see others walking in truth too. You have heard how the angels in heaven rejoice when they see one sinner repenting. Some of you have read it in the fifteenth chapter of Luke. Well, good people are like the angels in this - they are full of love and compassion, and when they see anyone turning away from sin, and doing what is right, it makes them feel happy.

Good people find walking in truth so pleasant, that they would like everybody else to walk in truth too. They do not wish to keep all this pleasantness to themselves, and to go to heaven alone. They want to see all about them loving Jesus Christ, and obeying Him, - all their relations, all their neighbours, all their old friends, all their young ones, indeed all the world. The more they see walking in truth, the more pleased they are.

Children, John was a good man, and full of love to souls, and this was one reason why he rejoiced.

(b) For another thing, John rejoiced *because it is very unusual to see children walking in truth.*

Dear children, I am very sorry to tell you there are many bad boys and girls in the world. Too many are careless, thoughtless, self-centred and disobedient. Nobody can rejoice over them.

I hear many fathers and mothers complaining about this. I hear many school teachers speak about it. I am afraid it is quite true.

There are many children who will not give their minds to anything that is good. They will not do what they are asked. They like to be lazy, and to have their own way. They love playing better than learning. They do things which God says are wicked and wrong and are not ashamed. And all this is very sad to see.

John, you may be sure, had found this out, for he was an old man as well as an Apostle, and had seen many things. He knew that even the children of good people sometimes turn out very badly. I dare say he remembered

Jacob and David, and all the sorrow their families caused them. And no doubt he knew what Solomon says in the book of Proverbs : "Foolishness is bound in the heart of a child."

When, therefore, John saw this lady's children not turning out badly, like others, but walking in the way they should go, he might well feel it was a special mercy. I am not at all surprised that he greatly rejoiced.

(c) John rejoiced *because he knew that walking in truth would make these children really happy in this life.*

John was not one of those foolish people who thought that being a Christian makes a person unhappy. John knew that the more love a person has for Jesus, the more happy they are.

John knew that life is always full of worry and trouble, and that the only way to get through life comfortably is to be a real follower and servant of Jesus Christ.

Dear children, remember what I say

this night: If ever you would be happy in this evil world, you must give your hearts to Jesus Christ, and follow Him. Give Him the entire charge of your souls, and ask Him to be your Saviour and your God ; and *then* you will be happy. Have no will of your own, and only try to please Him ; and *then* your life will be pleasant.

Trust all to Christ, and He will manage all that concerns your soul. Trust in Him at all times. Trust in Him in every condition - in sickness and in health, in youth and in old age, in poverty and in plenty, in sorrow and in joy. Trust in Him, and He will be a Shepherd to watch over you, a Guide to lead you, a King to protect you, a Friend to help you in time of need. Trust in Him, and He says Himself, "I will never leave thee nor forsake thee." He will put His Spirit into you, and give you a new heart. He will give you power to become a true child of God. He will give you grace to control your bad temper - to no longer be selfish - to love others as yourself. He will make your burdens lighter, and your work more easy. He will comfort you in time of trouble. Christ can make those happy who trust in Him. Christ died to save them, and Christ ever lives to give them peace.

Dear children, John was well aware of these things. He had learned them by experience. He saw this lady's children likely to be happy in this world, and no wonder he rejoiced.

(d) Lastly, John rejoiced *because he knew that walking in truth in the life that now is, would lead to glory and honour in the life to come.*

The life to come is the life we should all think most of. Many people seem only to care for what happens to them in this life. But they are sadly mistaken. This life is very short - it will soon be over. The oldest man will tell you it seems only a few years since he was a child. The life to come is the life of real importance; it will have no end; it will be never-ending happiness, or never-ending pain. Oh, what a serious thought that is!

Children, I do not doubt John was thinking of the life to come when he rejoiced. Our Lord Jesus Christ had often told him of the glorious rewards prepared for those who walk in truth. John thought of the rewards laid up in heaven for these children, and was glad.

I do not doubt that John looked forward in his heart to that day when Jesus shall come again. I dare say he saw in his mind's eye these dear children clothed in robes white as snow, having golden crowns on their heads, standing at Jesus Christ's right hand, enjoying pleasures for evermore. He saw them and their beloved mother meeting again in heaven, meeting in that blessed place where parting and sorrow shall be known no more.

Dear children, these must have been

sweet and pleasant thoughts. I do not wonder that John rejoiced.

And now I have finished what I have to say about our text. I have done what I promised. I have told you *what it is to walk in truth*. That is one thing. I have told you *why John rejoiced so much* to find this lady's children walking in truth. That is another.

Let me now wind up by saying something which, by God's help, may imprint this address in your minds. Alas, how many addresses are forgotten! I want this one to stick in your hearts, and do you good.

Ask yourselves then, every one of you, "Would John, if he knew me at this time, rejoice over me? Would John be pleased if he saw my ways and my behaviour, or would he look sorrowful and worried?"

O children, children do not neglect this question. This is no trivial matter. No wise man will ever rejoice over bad children. They may be clean and pretty, and have nice clothes, and look well *outwardly*, but a wise man will only feel sad when he sees them : he will feel they are wrong *inwardly*. They have not got new hearts, they are not going to heaven.

Believe me, it is far better to be good than to be pretty. It is far better to have grace in your hearts, than to have lots of money in your pockets, or fine clothes on your backs. None but children who love Christ are the children who rejoice a wise man's heart.

Beloved children, hear the last words I have to say to you. I give you all an invitation from Christ, my Master: I say to you in His name, *Come and walk in truth.*

This is the way to gladden the hearts of your parents and relations. This is the one thing above all others, which will please your ministers and teachers. You don't know how happy you make us, when you try to walk in truth. Then we know that all is well, even though we die and leave you behind us in this evil world. Then we know that your souls are safe, even though we are called away, and can help you and teach you no more. Then we know that you are prepared for troubles, however many may come upon you. For we know that walking in truth gives peace now, and we are sure that it leads to glory hereafter.

Come, then, this night, and begin to walk in truth. The devil will try to make you think it is too hard and that you cannot do it. Do not believe him: he is a liar. He wants to do you harm. Trust in Christ, and follow Him, you will soon say His way is a way of pleasantness, and a path of peace.

Pray for the Holy Spirit to come into your heart, and you will soon feel strong. He can guide you into all truth. Read the Bible regularly, and you will soon be made wise unto salvation. The Bible is the word of truth. Read and pray. Pray and read. Begin these habits, and keep them up. Do these things, and before long you will not say it is impossible to walk in truth. But *come, come at once*.

Children, I find Jesus Christ saying, in the third chapter of Revelation, "Behold I stand at the door and knock." Who knows but this may have been going on tonight? Who knows but Jesus may have been knocking at some of your hearts all through this sermon? If it be so, do not keep Him waiting any longer. If it be so, go to Him this night on your knees in prayer , go to Him and ask Him at once to come in. Ask Jesus to come and dwell in your heart, and take care of it as His own. Ask Him to put your name in His book of life . Ask Him to enable you to walk in truth.

Oh, think how many children in the world have never been invited as your are! How many boys and girls have never had the chance of being saved that you now enjoy. How many, perhaps, would leap for joy, and walk in truth at once, if they were invited. Beloved children, *take care*. You, at least, cannot say you were not invited. Jesus invites you: the Bible invites you: I, the servant of Christ, invite you all tonight. Oh, come to Christ! Come, and be happy.

Come and **WALK IN TRUTH.**

Little and Wise

"There be four things which are little upon the earth, but they are exceeding wise:

"The ants are a people not strong, yet they prepare their meat in the summer;

"The conies are but a feeble folk, yet make they their houses in the rocks;

"The locusts have no king, yet go they forth all of them by bands;

"The spider taketh hold with her hands, and is in kings' palaces."

PROVERBS 30. 24-28

Dear Children,

I should like you all to be very wise. Wisdom is far better than money or fine clothes, or grand houses, or horses and carriages. People who are not wise seldom get on well. They are seldom happy. My best wish for any dear boys and girls that I love is, that they may grow up very wise.

"But how are we to be wise?" some of you will ask. "What are we to do in order to get this wisdom, which you tell us is such a good thing?"

Dear children, if you would be wise, you must pray God to make you so. You must ask Him to put His Holy Spirit in your hearts, and give you wisdom. This is one thing.

Besides this, you must read God's holy book, the Bible. There you will find out what true wisdom is. There you will see what kind of things wise people do. This is another thing.

And now let me talk to you about the four verses in the Bible which I have looked out for you. They are verses which tell us about wisdom. I hope they will do you much good.

There you see that God tells you to learn a lesson from four little creatures - the ant, the cony, the locust, and the spider. He seems to say that they are all patterns of wisdom.

They are all poor little weak things. An ant is a little creeping insect, that everybody knows. A cony is a little creature very like a rabbit. A locust is like a large grasshopper. A spider is a thing that the smallest child need not be afraid of. But God tells you that the ant, the cony, the locust, and the spider, are very wise. Come then, dear children, and listen to me, while I tell you something about them. Some of you are only little now. But here you see it is possible to be little and yet wise.

(1) First of all, what are you to learn from the ants? You must learn from the

little ants to take thought about time to come.

"The ants," says the Bible, "prepare their meat in the summer." God has made the ants so wise and thoughtful, that they gather food in harvest time. They are not idle when the sun shines. They get all the grains of corn they can find, and lay them up in their nests. And so, when frost and snow come, the ants are not starved. They stay snug in their nests, and have plenty to eat.

The butterflies are much prettier to look at than the ants. They have beautiful wings, and make a much finer show. But the butterflies, poor things, are not so wise as the ants. They fly among the flowers, and enjoy themselves all summer. They never think of gathering food for the winter. When the winter comes the butterflies all die, whilst the ants stay alive.

And now, I want you each to learn wisdom from the ants. I want you, like them, to think of the future.

You have each got within you a soul that will live for ever. Your body will die some time. Your soul never will. And your soul needs thought and care as much as your body. It needs to have its sins pardoned. It needs grace to make it please God. It needs power to be good. It needs to have God for its best friend, in order to be happy.

And, dear children, the best time for seeking pardon, grace, and the friendship of God, is in your youth. Youth and childhood are your summer. Now you are strong and well. Now you have plenty of time. Now you have few worries and troubles to distract you. Now is the best time for laying up food for your souls.

Ah, my beloved children, you must remember that winter is before you! Old age is your winter. Your frost, and snow, and rain, and storms, are all yet to come. Sorrow, pain, sickness, death and judgment, will all come with old age. Happy are those who get ready for it in good time. Happy are those who, like the ants, take thought for things to come!

They are wise boys and girls who read their Bibles, and learn many texts by heart. They are wise boys and girls who pray to God every day to give them His Holy Spirit. They are wise who remember what their parents and teachers tell them, and try hard to be good. They are wise who dislike all bad ways, and bad words, and always tell the truth. Such boys and girls are like the little ants. They are laying up stores for the time to come.

Dear children, if you have not done so before, I hope you will begin to do so now. If you have done so, I hope you will keep on doing so, and do so more and more. Do not be like the foolish butterflies. Be like the ants. Think of the time to come, and be wise.

(2) But let us now go on and see what you are to learn of the conies. You must learn of the little conies to have a

place of safety to run to in time of danger.

"The conies," says the Bible, "make their houses in the rocks." The conies are like little rabbits and they are afraid of foxes, dogs and cruel men, who hunt and kill them. They are poor, weak things, and are not strong enough to fight and take care of themselves. So what do they do? They make their holes among stones and rocks, whenever they can. They go where men cannot dig them out. They go where dogs and foxes cannot follow them. And then, they run away into those holes, and are safe.

The hare can run much faster than the cony, for it has much longer legs. The stag is much bigger than the cony, and has got fine horns. But the hare and the stag have got no holes to run into. They lie out on the open fields. And so when men come to hunt them with dogs and guns, they are soon caught and killed. But the little cony has a hiding-place to run to, and in this way he often escapes.

Now, dear children, I want you to learn wisdom from the little conies. I want you to have a place of safety for your souls.

Your souls have many enemies. You are in danger from many things which may do them harm. You have each of you a wicked heart within you. Have you not often found how hard it is to be good? You have each a terrible enemy, seeking to ruin you for ever, and take you to hell. That enemy is the devil. You cannot see him. But he is never far off. You are each living in a world where there are many bad people, and few good. Dear children, all these things are against you.

You need the help of One who can keep you safe. You need a hiding-place for your precious souls. You need a dear Friend, who is able to save you from your evil hearts, from the devil, and from the bad example of wicked people. Listen to me, and I will tell you about Him.

There is One who is able to keep your souls quite safe. His name is Jesus Christ. He is strong enough to save you, for He is God's own Son. He is willing to save you, for He came down from heaven and died upon the cross for your sakes. And he loves all children. He liked to have them with Him when He was upon the earth. He took them up in His arms and blessed them.

Dear children, those boys and girls are wise who put their trust in Jesus Christ, and ask Him to take care of their souls. Such boys and girls will be kept safe. Jesus Christ loves them. Jesus Christ will not let them come to harm. He will not allow the devil, or wicked people, to ruin their souls.

Jesus is the true rock for children to run to. Boys and girls who trust Him will be cared for while they live, and go to heaven when they die. Jesus is the true hiding-place. Boys and girls who love Him will be safe and happy.

Dear children, I hope you will all try to have your souls kept safe. Do not put off asking the Lord Jesus Christ to take care of them. Do not say to yourselves, "Oh, we shall have plenty of time by and by!" Who knows what may happen to you before long. Perhaps you may be sick and ill. Perhaps you may lose all your kind friends and be left alone. Oh, go and pray to Jesus now! Be like the wise little conies. Get a safe hiding-place for your soul.

(3) Let us now see what you are to learn of the locusts. You must learn of the locusts to love one another, to keep together, and help one another.

"The locusts," says the Bible, "have no king, yet go they forth all of them in bands." They have nobody over them to tell them what to do. They are poor little weak insects by themselves. One locust alone can do very little. The least boy or girl would kill a locust, if he were to tread on it. It would be dead at once.

But the little locusts are so wise that they always keep together. They fly about in such numbers that you could not count them, you would think they were a black cloud. They do not quarrel with one another. They help each other. In this way the locusts are able to do a very great deal. They make the farmers and gardeners quite afraid when they are seen coming. They eat up the grass and corn. They strip all the leaves off the trees. And this is because they help one another.

Dear children, I want you to learn from the little locusts always to love one another, and never to quarrel. You should try to be kind and good-natured to other boys and girls. You should make it a rule never to be selfish, never to be spiteful, never to get into a fit of rage, never to fight with one another. Boys and girls who do such things are not wise. They are more foolish than the locusts.

Dear children, quarrelling is very wicked. It pleases the devil, for he is always trying to make people wicked, like himself. It does not please God, for God is love. Selfishness and quarrelling are most improper in Christian children. They should try to be like Christ. Christ was never selfish. He didn't set out to please Himself.

Think what a great deal of good boys and girls might do, if they would be like the little locusts, and love one another. Think how useful they might be to their fathers and mothers: they might save them much trouble, and help in many little ways. Think what a great deal of money they might collect to help missionaries. If every child in England was to save some of their pocket money for missionaries, it would be a large sum of money. Think, above all, what good boys and girls might do, if they agreed to pray for one another. How happy they would be! Such prayers would be heard.

Dear children, as long as you live, love one another. Try to be of one mind. Have nothing to do with quarrelling and fighting. Hate it, and think of it as a great sin. You ought to agree together far better than the little locusts. They have no king to teach them. You have a King who has promised His Spirit to teach you, and that King is Christ. Oh, be wise like the locusts, and love one another!

(4) And now, last of all, let us see what you are to learn from the spider. You must learn from the spider not to give up trying to be good because of a little trouble.

"The spider," says the Bible, "taketh hold with her hands, and is in king's palaces." The spider is a poor little feeble thing, you all know. But the spider takes great pains in making her web. The spider creeps even into grand houses, and climbs to the top of the finest rooms. And there she spins her web. There seems no keeping her out. People come and brush the web away but the spider sets to work at once, and makes it again new. No insect is so persevering as the spider. She does her work over and over again. She will not give up.

I remember a story of a great king who got back his kingdom by taking example from a spider. Poor man, he had been driven away from his kingdom, like David, by wicked rebels. He had tried often to get his kingdom back. He had fought many battles, but had always been beaten.

At last he began to think it was no use: he would give up and fight no more. It happened at that time that he was lying awake in bed very early one summer's morning, when he saw a spider at work. The spider was trying to make a thread from one side of the room to the other. Twelve times she tried in vain: twelve times the thread broke, and she fell to the ground. Twelve times she got up, and tried again. But she did not give up: she persevered, and the thirteenth time she succeeded. Now when the king saw that, he said to himself, "Why should I not persevere too, in trying to get back my kingdom? Why should I not succeed at last, though I have so often failed?"

He did try again. He succeeded. He conquered his cruel enemies, and got back his kingdom. Dear children, this king's name was Robert Bruce. He got back his kingdom, in Scotland, by copying the spider.

Now I want you to make the spider's example a pattern for your souls. I want you, like the spider, to persevere in sticking to what is good. I should like you to be determined that you will never give up. I want you to keep on trying not to do what is evil, and trying always to do what is good, and pleasing to God.

Ah, dear children, it is a wicked world, I am sorry to say ; and there are many who will try hard to make you wicked, as you grow up. The devil will try hard to make you forget God. Bad men and women will tell you there is no need for you to be so good.

I beg you not to give way. I beseech you to persevere. Keep on praying every day ; keep on reading your Bibles regularly ; keep on regularly going to Church on Sunday. Alas, there are many boys and girls who give up everything that is good, as soon as they leave school. While they are at school they use their Bibles, and hymn-books, and prayer-books. When they stop going to school, they stop using all their books too. They often get into bad company ; they often take up bad ways; they often go idling about all Sunday. They seem to forget all that has been taught them. This is not persevering. This is being more foolish than the little spider. It is wicked and unwise.

Dear children, there is a glorious house in heaven, where I hope I shall see some of you. There is a palace there, belonging to Jesus Christ, far finer than any palace on earth, in which all Jesus Christ's people shall live and be happy for ever and ever. Dear children, I hope I shall see many of you there.

But, remember, if you and I are to meet in this glorious palace, you must persevere, and be careful about your souls. You must pray heartily. You must read your Bibles regularly. You must fight against sin daily. You must say when bad people entice you to do wrong, "I will not give up following Christ : I will try to please Him." Oh, let the little spider be your pattern all your lives! Persevere and be wise.

And now, I will finish by asking you to think of what I have been telling you.

I have told you of four little creatures, which are very wise: the ants, the conies, the locusts and the spiders. I have shown you that the ants are a pattern of wisdom, because they think of time to come. The conies are a pattern of wisdom, because they make their houses in safe places. The locusts are a pattern of wisdom, because they help one another. The spiders are a pattern of wisdom, because they persevere. Dear children, I want you to be like them. Some of you may possibly never live to be men and women. But one thing you may be, even now: you may be wise.

Be wise, like the ants. Consider these two verses of the Bible, and learn them by heart. "Remember now thy Creator in the days of thy youth." (Eccles. 12. 1) "Prepare to meet thy God." (Amos 4. 12)

Be wise, like the conies. Consider these two verses of the Bible, and learn them by heart. "Believe on the Lord Jesus Christ, and thou shalt be saved." (Acts 16. 31) "Thou art my hiding-place; thou shalt preserve me from trouble." (Psa. 32. 7)

Be wise, like the locusts. Consider these two verses of the Bible, and learn them by heart. "By this shall all men know that ye are My disciples, if ye have love one to another." (John 13. 35) "He that loveth not his brother whom he hath seen, how can he love God whom he hath not seen?" (I John 4. 20)

Be wise, like the spiders. Consider these words of the Bible, and learn them by heart. "Ask, and it shall be given you : seek, and ye shall find." (Matt. 7. 7) "Let us lay aside every weight, and the sin which doth so easily beset us : and let us run with patience the race that is set before us, looking unto Jesus." (Heb. 12. 1-2)

Dear children, think on these things. This is the way to be happy and wise.

Never forget what God says in the Bible : "Better is a poor and a wise child, than an old and foolish king." (Eccles. 4. 13.) "The wise shall inherit glory." (Prov. 3. 35.)

No More Crying!

"God shall wipe away all tears from their eyes ; and there shall be no more death, neither sorrow, nor crying, neither shall there be any more pain."

REVELATION 21. 4.

Beloved Children,

I should like you to read the Bible text from Revelations twice over. I am going to tell you something which, I hope, will make you remember that text as long as you live.

I am going to tell you about three places, of which the Bible says a great deal. It doesn't matter what we know about some places ; but it matters a lot to know something about the three places of which I am now going to speak.

(1) There is a place where there is a great deal of crying.

(2) There is a place where there is nothing else but crying.

(3) There is a place where there is no crying at all.

Now, listen to me, and I will tell you a few things worth knowing.

(1) First of all, there is a place where there is a great deal of crying.

What is that place? It is the world in which you and I live. It is a world full of beautiful and pleasant things. The sun shining by day and the stars by night; the blue hills looking up to heaven, and the rolling sea ebbing and flowing; the broad quiet lakes, and the rushing restless rivers; the flowers blooming in the spring, and the fields full of corn in autumn; the birds singing in the woods, and the lambs playing in the meadows - all these are beautiful things. I could look at them for hours and say, "What a beautiful world it is!" But still it is a world where there is a great deal of crying. It is a world where there are many tears.

There was "crying" in Bible times. Hagar wept when she thought Ishmael was dying ; Abraham mourned when Sarah died ; Joseph wept when his brothers sold him into Egypt ; David wept when Absalom was killed. There was weeping at Jerusalem when good king Josiah was killed in battle. There was weeping at Bethlehem when Herod killed all the little children who were not more than two years old. These things, and many like them, you will find in your Bibles.

There is "crying" now all over the world. Little babies cry when they want anything or feel pain. Boys and girls cry when they are hurt, or frightened, or disciplined. Grown-up people cry sometimes when they are in trouble, or when they see those die whom they love. In short, wherever there is sorrow and pain, there is "crying."

I dare say you have seen people come to church all dressed in black. That is called being in mourning. Some relation or friend of these people has died, and therefore they dress in black. Well, remember when you see people in mourning, somebody has been "crying."

I dare say you have seen graves in church-yards, and have heard that when people die, they are buried there.

Some of them are very little graves, no longer than you are. Well, remember that when those graves were made, and little coffins were let down into them, there was "crying."

Children, did you ever think what all this crying came from? Did you ever consider how it first began? Did you ever hear how weeping and tears came into the world? God did not make crying - that is certain. All that God made was "very good." Listen to me, and I will tell you how "crying" began.

Crying came into the world because of sin. Sin is the cause of all the weeping, and tears, and sorrow, and pain, which there are upon earth. All the crying began when Adam and Eve ate the forbidden fruit and became sinners. It was sin which brought pain and sickness and death into the world. It was sin which brought into the world selfishness, and unkindness, and quarrelling, and stealing, and fighting. If there had been no wickedness, there would have been no weeping. If there had been so sin, there would have been no "crying."

See now, my beloved children, how much you ought to hate sin. All the unhappiness in the world came from sin. How strange and wonderful it is that any one can take pleasure in sin! Do not let that be the case with you. Watch against sin. Fight with it. Avoid it. Do not listen to it. Take the advice of St. Paul : "Abhor that which is evil." Take the advice of Solomon : "When sinners entice thee, consent thou not." Say to yourself every morning, "Sin caused crying, and so I will hate sin."

See, again, my beloved children, how foolish it is to expect perfect happiness in this world. It is expecting what you will not find. The world is a place where there is much "crying," and where things do not always go on pleasantly. I hear many boys and girls talking of pleasures they will have when they are men and women. I am sorry for them when I hear them talking in this way. I know they are mistaken. I know they will be disappointed. They will find when they grow up, that they cannot get through the world without many troubles and problems. There are no roses without thorns. There are no years without dark and rainy days. There is no living on earth without "crying" and tears.

(2) I will now speak of the second place which I promised to tell you about. There is a place where there is nothing else but "crying."

What is that place? It is the place to which people go when they are dead, if they have not believed in Jesus. It is the place which the Bible calls hell. In hell there is no laughter and smiling. There is nothing but "weeping and wailing and gnashing of teeth." In hell there is no happiness. Those who go there cry all night and day without stopping. They have no rest. They never go to sleep and wake up happy.

They never stop crying in hell.

Beloved children, I am sorry to tell you that there are many people going to hell. "Broad is the way that leadeth unto destruction, and many there be which go in it." I am afraid that many children are going to hell. Many boys and girls are so naughty and ill-behaved, that I am sure they are not fit for heaven. And if they are not fit for heaven, where will they go if they die? There is only one other place to which they can go. They must go to hell.

It makes me sad to say these things. I cannot bear the thought of boys and girls going to that dreadful place where there is nothing but crying. My heart's desire and prayer to God for you is, that you may not go to hell. But I want you to know some things which you must take notice of so as to be sure that you do not go to hell. Listen to me now while I ask you a few questions.

For one thing, I will ask you - do you love Jesus Christ? You ought to love Him. He died for your sins upon the cross, that He might save you from hell. He allowed Himself to be shut up in the dark prison of the grave, that your sins might be forgiven, and that you might not be chained in hell for ever. Think about this! If you love nothing but play and eating and drinking and fine clothes and story-books and do not love Christ, you are not in the right way. If you do not take care, you will go at last to the place where there is nothing but "crying."

I will ask you another thing - do you try to please Christ? You ought to do so. I read in the Bible that Jesus Christ said, "If ye love Me, keep my commandments." - "Ye are my friends, if ye do whatsoever I command you." Dear children, think about this! If you are selfish, or angry, or tell lies, or quarrel with one another, or do not do as you are told, you are not Christ's friends. Take care. If you do not take care, you will go at last to the place where there is nothing but "crying."

I will ask you another thing - do you keep the Sunday holy? You ought to do so. God commands it, and it is for your good. I once heard of a little boy who went to play on the ice on Sunday, instead of going to church.

"Tommy," said his mother, "why did you do that?"

"Mother," said Tommy, "I did not remember that it was Sunday."

"Tommy," said his mother, "that is the very thing God told you not to do. He said in the fourth commandment, 'Remember to keep holy the Sabbath.'"

Dear children, think about this! If you do not like to give God one day in the week, your hearts are not right. Take care. If you do not take care, you will go at last to the place where there is nothing but "crying."

I will ask you another thing - do you say your prayers? You ought to. God will never be a friend to you if you do not speak to Him, and ask Him to take care of your soul and make you good. If you never pray, or say your prayers without thinking, your heart will soon be full of mischief and sin. It will never be empty for a day.

I once heard of a boy who had a little garden given to him all full of flowers. But he didn't care for it. He never raked it or weeded it. After a few weeks, the weeds came up so thick that the flowers died. Dear children, think of this! If you do not ask God to put the Holy Spirit in your hearts, the devil will soon fill them with sin. Take care. If you do not take care, you will go at last to the place where there is nothing but "crying."

I will ask you one more question - do you read your Bible ? You ought to do so. That beautiful book is able to keep you from hell and save your soul. If you use the Bible rightly you will not be hurt by the devil.

I once heard of a little boy in Africa, who was sleeping with his father in the open air, near a fire. He awoke in the middle of the night and saw a great lion close to him, looking as if he was going to seize him. The little boy took up a lighted stick out of the fire, and put it in the lion's face, and drove him away.

Dear children, think of this ! The devil is "a roaring lion seeking whom he may devour." But he cannot harm you if you make a right use of the Bible. If you would drive him from you you must read your Bible. If you can read, and yet neglect your Bible, you are in great danger. Take care. If you do not take care the devil will carry you off to the place where there is nothing but "crying."

Beloved children, remember my five questions. Think of them often, and test your own hearts by asking these questions. I am not afraid for children who love Jesus, and try to please Him, and keep the Sunday holy, and pray and read their Bibles. I am not afraid that they will go to hell if they die. But

I am afraid for children who care nothing about these things. I think they are in great danger.

(3) I will now speak of the third place about which I promised to tell you something. There is a place where there is no crying at all.

What is this place? It is heaven. It is the place people go to when they are dead, if they have believed in Jesus. There, all is joy and happiness. There, no tears are shed. There, sorrow, pain, sickness and death can never enter in. There is no crying there because there is nothing that causes grief.

Dear children, there will be no more lessons in heaven. All will have been learned. The school will be closed. There will be no need for rules or discipline. There will be an eternal holiday.

There will be no more work in heaven. Man will no longer need to labour for his bread. The head will no longer have to ache with thinking. The hands will no longer be stiff and sore from hard work. There will be an eternal rest for the people of God.

There will be no sickness in heaven. Pain and disease and weakness and death will not be known. The people who dwell there shall no more say, "I am sick." They will be always well. There will be nothing but health and strength for evermore.

There will be no sin in heaven. There will be no bad tempers, no unkind words, no spiteful actions. The great tempter, the devil, will not be allowed to come in and spoil the happiness. There shall be nothing but holiness and love for evermore.

Best of all, the Lord Jesus Christ himself will be in the midst of heaven. His people shall at last see Him face to face, and will never need to leave His presence. He shall gather His lambs into His arms, and wipe away all tears from all eyes. Where He is will be fulness of joy, and at His right hand shall be pleasures for evermore.

Would you like to go to heaven? We cannot live always in this world. A day will come when we must die, like the people who have died already. Would you like to go to heaven when you die? Listen to me, and I will tell you something about the way by which you must go to get to heaven.

If you would go to heaven, you must have your sins forgiven, and your hearts made new and good. There is only One who can do this for you. That one is the Lord Jesus Christ. God has appointed Him to be the Friend of sinners. He can wash away your sins in His own precious blood. He can make your hearts new by putting the Holy Spirit in them. He is the Way and the Door into heaven. He has the keys in His hand. Children, if you want to go to heaven, you must ask Jesus Christ to let you in.

Ask Jesus in prayer to get a place ready for you in that world where there is no "crying." Ask Him to put your name in His book of life, and to make you one of His people. Ask Him to cleanse you from all your sins, and to put the Holy Ghost in your heart. Ask Him to give you power to fight His battle against sin, the world, and the devil. Ask Him to give you grace to make you good while you are young, and good when you grow up, that so you may be safe while you live, and happy for ever when you die.

Children, Jesus Christ is ready to do all this, if you will only ask Him. He has done it for many people already. He is waiting to do it for you at this very time. Do not be afraid to ask Him. Tell Him you have heard that He was very kind to people when He was on earth, and ask Him to be kind to you. Remind Him how kind He was to the poor dying thief on the cross. Say to Him, "Lord Jesus, remember ; I want to go to heaven. Lord, think upon me. Lord, give me the Holy Spirit. Lord, pardon my sins, and give me a new heart. Lord Jesus, save me."

And now, children, I have kept my word. I have told you of three places:-

(1) I have told you of a place where there is nothing but crying. I hope none of you will go there.

(2) I have told you of a place where there is no crying. I hope you will all go there.

(3) I have told you of a place where there is a great deal of crying. That place is the world in which you are living.

Would you like, last of all, to know the best way to be happy in this world? Listen to me, and I will tell you.

The happiest people in this world are those who make the Bible the rule of their lives. They read their Bibles often. They believe what the Bible says. They love that Saviour Jesus Christ of whom the Bible speaks. They try to obey what the Bible commands. None are so happy as these people. They cannot prevent sickness and trouble coming to them sometimes. But they learn from the Bible to bear them patiently. Children, if you would get through the world happily, make the Bible your best friend.

Shall I tell you a story that I once heard about a little boy and the Bible? Perhaps it will help you to remember what I have just been saying. I want the words I have just written to stick for ever in your minds.

"Father," said this little boy one day, "I do not see any use in reading the Bible. I do not see that it does people any good." Little Johnny said this in a rather cross and sulky way, and his father thought it best not to begin reasoning with him. "Johnny," he said, "put on your hat and come out, and take a walk with me."

Johnny's father took him first to a house where there was an old woman who was very poor, and he talked to her about her poverty. "Sir," said the old woman, "I do not complain. I have read in the Bible these words, 'I have learned in whatsoever state I am therewith to be content.'"

"Johnny," said the little boy's father, "hear what the old woman says."

They went on to another house, where there was a young woman who was very ill, and never likely to get better. Johnny's father asked her if she felt afraid to die. "No!" she said, "I find it written in the Bible, 'Though I walk through the valley of the shadow of death I will fear no evil, for Thou art with me.'"

"Johnny," said the little boy's father again, "hear what the young woman says."

Children, when Johnny and his father came home that afternoon from their walk, his father asked him one question, "Johnny," he said, "do you think it is of any use to read the Bible? Do you think reading the Bible does people any good?"

And now what do you think Johnny said? I will tell you. He hung down his head, and said nothing. But his face got very red, and he looked very much ashamed.

Children, from that very day Johnny was never heard again to say, "It is of no use reading the Bible."

Beloved children, remember my parting words. The way to get through the world with the least possible crying, is to read the Bible, believe the Bible, pray over the Bible, live by the Bible.

Those who go through life in this way will have the least "crying" in this world. And best of all, he will have no crying at all in the world to come.

The Happy Little Girl

"But godliness with contentment is great gain."

1 TIMOTHY 6.6

Dear Children,

Would you like to know who was the happiest child I ever saw? Listen to me, and I will tell you.

The happiest child I ever saw was a little girl whom I once met travelling in a railway carriage. We were both going on a journey to London, and we travelled a great many miles together. She was only eight years old, and she was blind. She had never been able to see at all. She had never seen the sun, the stars, the sky, the grass, the flowers, the trees, the birds and all those pleasant things which you see every day of your lives ; but still she was quite happy.

She was by herself, poor little thing. She had no friends or relations to take care of her on the journey, and be good to her ; but she was quite happy and content. She said when she got into the carriage, "Tell me how many people there are in the carriage: I am blind, and can see nothing."

A gentleman asked her, "Are you not afraid?"

"No," she said, "I am not frightened ; I have travelled before, and I trust in God, and people are always very good to me."

But I soon found out why she was so happy ; and what do you think it was? She loved Jesus Christ, and Jesus Christ loved her ; she had sought Jesus Christ, and she had found Him!

I began to talk to her about the Bible, and I soon saw she knew a great deal of it. She went to a school where the teacher used to read the Bible to her; and she was a good girl, and had remembered what her teacher had read.

Dear children, you cannot think how many things in the Bible this poor little blind girl knew. I only wish that every grown up person in England knew as much as she did. But I must try and tell you some of them.

She talked to me about sin, how it first came into the world when Adam and Eve ate the forbidden fruit, and how it was to be seen everywhere now. "Oh," she said, "there are no really good people ! The very best people in the world commit many sins every day, and I am sure we all waste a great deal of time even if we do nothing else wrong. Oh, we are all such sinners ! There is nobody who has not sinned a great many sins."

And then she talked about Jesus Christ. She told me about the agony in the garden of Gethsemane, about His sweating drops of blood, about the soldiers nailing Him to the cross, about the spear piercing His side and blood and water coming out. "Oh," she said, "how very good it was of Him to die for us, and such a cruel death! How good He was to suffer so for our sins."

And then she talked to me about wicked people. She told how she was afraid there were a great many in the world, and it made her very unhappy to see how many of her school-friends and acquaintances acted. "But," she said, "I know why they are so wicked: it is because they do not try to be good, they do not wish to be good, they do not ask Jesus to make them good."

I asked her what part of the Bible she liked best. She told me she liked the story of Jesus Christ, but the chapters she was most fond of were the last three chapters of the Book of Revelation. I had got a Bible with me, and I took it out and read these chapters to her as we went along.

When I had finished she began to talk about heaven. "Think," she said, "how nice it will be to be there! There will be no sorrow, crying, or tears. Jesus Christ will be there, for it says, 'the Lamb is the light thereof,' and we shall always be with Him; and there shall be no night there. They will need no candle nor light of the sun."

Dear children, just think of this poor little blind girl. Think of her taking pleasure in talking of Jesus Christ. Think of her rejoicing in the passage about heaven, where there shall be no sorrow nor night.

I have never seen her since. She went to her own home in London, and I do not know whether she is alive or not; but I hope she is, and I have no doubt Jesus Christ has taken good care of her.

Dear children, are you as happy and as cheerful as she was? You are not blind. You have eyes, and can run about and see everything, and go where you like, and read as much as you please to yourselves. But are you as happy as this poor little girl?

Oh, if you wish to be happy in this world, remember my advice today and do as the little blind girl did: "Love Jesus Christ, and He will love you ; seek Him early, and you shall find Him."

Little Things

"He that is faithful in that which is least is faithful also in much ..."

LUKE 16.10

Dear Children,

Did you ever see a bird's nest? Did you ever look closely at it? Did you ever observe how wisely and cleverly it is made? There are few things so beautiful and well-built as a bird's nest.

Millions of nests are made by fully grown birds every year. Millions of young birds are hatched and reared in them. There would soon be no more thrushes, larks and nightingales, if there were no nests.

The most beautiful bird's nest I ever saw was made of stone and timber, and not of twigs and moss. It was not made by the beaks and claws of birds, but by the hands of men. Children, what kind of nest do you think this was? I am sure you will never guess, and so I must tell you.

The bird's nest which I thought so beautiful is a large house in Ireland, at a place called Kingstown. It is a house built by kind people to take in boys and girls who have no friends or family. Once received into this house these boys and girls are washed, and clothed, and fed, and taught, until they are old enough to make their own living. Children, do you not think the "Bird's Nest" was a very good name to give to this house?

Now, it costs a great deal of money to keep up this "Bird's Nest" in proper order. The clothes the poor, friendless boys and girls wear cost money; the food that they eat every day costs money; the teachers who teach them every day must be paid for their work; the servants who help to keep the place clean must have their wages; the house itself must be kept in repair. All this costs a great deal of money. Children, shall I tell you how some of this money is raised?

Some of the money which goes to keep up the Kingstown "Bird's Nest" is collected by little boys and girls in

Dublin, who ask their friends to help. Think what a nice thing that is to do! How much better to collect money for the "Bird's Nest," than to waste it on sweeties, and cakes, and toys!

Children, when I was over in Dublin, I saw these little collectors of money for the "Bird's Nest" gathered together. It was a very pleasant sight to my eyes to see so many little friends to the friendless, and helpers of the helpless. I gave them a speech to encourage them and cheer them on. The address which I will now share with you is part of that speech. I hope it will do you good.

My dear children,

I have been asked to speak to the boys and girls who collect for the Kingstown "Bird's Nest." I must begin by telling you that it is a very hard thing to do. I must get you all to help me. How can you help me? You can help me by being as quiet and attentive as you can, by sitting as still as you can, and by opening your ears as wide as you can.

Children, what is the first thing we want to do for the boys and girls in the "Bird's Nest"? I will tell you.

Our *great* work is to help them to get to heaven. We want their souls to be saved by faith in the Lord Jesus Christ. We want them to be washed in Jesus' blood, clothed in His robe of righteousness, and made partakers of His grace. We want them to grow up holy, praying, Bible-teaching, God-fearing, men and women.

But some people may say, "What have boys and girls to do with this 'Bird's Nest'? Why not leave it to the grown people to get all the money? They are better able to do it. Boys and girls should not have anything to do with it."

Why, dear boys and girls, there are no persons in the world that are so bound to work for the Lord Jesus Christ, and for the souls of people, as children. There are none who ought to try so much to make known the Gospel of Jesus Christ as children. Do you know what happens to children in heathen lands? Here in this country when boys and girls are born there is normally great joy and pleasure but that isn't always the case in other countries in the world.

You have heard of the South Sea Islands. Look at the map of the world. Those little black dots to the left of South America, they are the South Sea Islands. Well, many years ago these islands were full of people who had not heard of Jesus. The poor people there bowed down to worship gods made of sticks and stones, and knew nothing of the Lord Jesus Christ.

Kind missionaries went to them, and told them of Christ, and salvation by Him. God blessed their work and many of the people were converted, and many of these heathen islands have now become Christian lands. After they were converted, many of the people said, "We wish we had heard these things before! If you had only told us these things long ago, we should never have done the wicked things we did."

At one of these islands, a woman got up after a missionary meeting, and said, "Oh, sir, if I had only heard these things before! I had nineteen little children, and have murdered every one of them! Because I knew nothing of the Bible, I didn't care for my dear little children. Oh, that I had known long ago about Jesus Christ and about this blessed Bible, and about the way to Heaven!" I always say that *women, children,* and the *poor,* ought to do more for the Gospel than any others in the world. It brings *them* so many blessings.

But now comes the question: What can you do?

Many people will say, "Well, what can these little boys and girls do? What is the use of such little help as they can give to the 'Bird's Nest' and other good causes?"

Oh, my dear children, who can tell the power of *littles*? The power of *littles* is very wonderful! No one knows what can be done by a *little*, and a *little*, and a *little* more.

Did you every think about Noah's Ark? Did you ever think what a large thing Noah's Ark must have been? Just think of Noah having to make a vessel big enough to hold *all* the animals and *all* the birds. How do you think the ark was made? It was not done all at once. Oh, no! It was made plank by plank, and piece by piece, by little and little. Perhaps you would have said, if you had seen Noah at his work, "Oh, what's the use of that little piece, such a tiny bit?" or "What's the use of that one plank?" Children, *little* by *little* is that which makes a large thing at last. So we want as many little things as you can give to good causes and joined together, they will make the whole of what is needed.

God says in the Bible, "Who hath despised the day of small things?" There is also a text spoken by our Lord Jesus Christ about little things. "He that is faithful in that which is least, is faithful also in much ; and he that is unjust in the least, is unjust also in much." The real Christian must be faithful in little things as well as in great things.

Let me tell you a story of a man who knew the value of little things. This man became one of the most important people in the city of Paris, the capital city of France.

Well, this man came to Paris when he was a boy, a little boy, not bigger than many of you. When he came there he wanted someone to find him something to do. Poor little fellow, he asked one man after another, could they give him some work? He was greatly discouraged, and almost tired of saying "Please, sir, can you give me something to do?" and of hearing the answer, "No: I have nothing for you to do; what can such a little fellow as you do?"

At last one day he went into a banker's house. There were many people standing in the office, so he went up to one and said, "Please, sir, can you find me something to do?" "No: I cannot," was the answer.

As he went to the door to go on his way, he saw a pin on the floor. He stooped down and picked it up, and stuck it in his sleeve. The chief person in the office saw him do this, and called him back. "Boy," he said, "what did you pick up that pin for? I don't want it, it would be of no value to me, but I want to know what made you pick it up."

"Well, sir," said the boy, "I will tell you. My mother told me never to waste little things, but always to take care of them ! She said, 'My son, if you will take care of little things, even of pins, you will always find some use for them.' I always like to do what my mother told me. I love my mother, and I always take care of little things."

These words struck the banker so much that he said, "My boy, come to me tomorrow morning." He did so, and the gentleman gave him a place in the bank. He turned out to be so steady and diligent, that he soon rose from one thing to another, and in time he became the highest partner in the firm, and when he died he was the richest man in all Paris. His name was Laffitte.

See what great results come from picking up a little pin. It showed character. It showed what the boy was. He was a boy that minded *little things*, and all his success in life afterwards he traced to this little circumstance.

Little things are never to be despised. I always tell my own boys never to think lightly of every-day things. Oh, the importance of little habits! Habits of reading, habits of prayer, habits at meals, little habits through the day - all are little things. But they make up the character, and are of the utmost importance. So, dear children, when people tell you there is no use in little helpers like you, don't mind them. By attending to *little things*, you will be able to do much to support God's work everywhere.

Now what can you do?

(1) *Take a deep interest in the whole concern.*

For example, the "Bird's Nest" teaches these boys and girls to be clean, to work, to behave well, to read the Bible and to know the way to heaven. What a great work this is! What an honour to be a helper of it!

I know a clergyman who was once going to a missionary meeting, and he met a boy running in a very great hurry. So he stopped him, and said,

"My boy, why are you running so fast? What is the matter?"

"Oh sir," said the boy, "I am going to a missionary meeting, and I must not lose a minute, for I am late."

"But what makes you in such a hurry about it? They are not waiting for you."

"Oh," said the boy, "I am part of the concern."

"How is that?" said the clergyman.

"Why, sir, it's a thing that I support, and I have a share in it myself."

So off he ran to the meeting, and the clergyman followed. The Report was read, and the gentleman who read it out, read that the total sum of money collected was so many pounds and *one penny*. "Oh," said the boy, "there goes my penny!" Giving the penny made him feel that he was part of the concern.

(2) *Always pray about missionary work.*

If God's blessing is to be got, it must be sought. It is of great importance that all children should pray for God's blessing on every work they enter into.

One of our missionaries came home from India, and told us that as he was going home one night, he passed by some trees and heard voices. He thought he would like to hear what was going on and to his great joy he heard the voices of children praying.

These Indian children were praying for a blessing upon the missionary work. He heard one child pray, "Oh Lord, I pray Thee to make my grandmother's ears longer."

Does anyone here know what he meant by that prayer? He meant that as his grandmother did not believe in Christ Jesus, her heart was unchanged. She would not listen to what she was told about Christ, or she would pay no attention to what she heard. So her little grandson prayed that she might have longer ears because he thought it would help her to listen more carefully to what the missionary said!

Dear children, pray that God would make people's ears a great deal longer. People are told about missionary work. You talk to them about the work that goes on at the "Bird's Nest" or other missions. You ask them to help you to give something to support God's work. But you sometimes speak to them in vain. Their ears are so short that they will not listen, or do not understand what you mean.

Pray that the hearts of these people may be touched, so that more donations may come in, that more helpers may be found, and that God's work may go on faster and faster?

(3) One thing more I will say. Let me beg of you to help God's cause by showing *a missionary spirit at home*.

I would not like to hear of any boys or girls being helpers of God's work, while they don't show a loving and kind spirit in their own homes, towards their fathers, and mothers, and sisters, and brothers.

My dear children, every one of you should be a missionary at home. Try to be a Christian at home. Strive to be like the Lord Jesus Christ. Keep His words in your minds. Walk in His steps in your own families, towards your fathers and mothers and with every one else.

There is a commandment I often think of, about which a great man once said a curious thing. There was in this country, before you or I, or any one now living, was born, a great man called Archbishop Usher: a holy, godly, Christian Archbishop.

This Archbishop resolved one day to pay a visit to a very holy Scottish minister, called Rutherford. He wanted to see him in his private life and how he was with his family. So he went dressed as a common labourer, so that they might not know who he was.

Usher knocked at the door, and asked very quietly for a night's lodging. Mr. Rutherford was a good, kind man and was in the habit of receiving strangers into his house. So the door was opened, and Usher was allowed to have the night's lodging. He was sent to the kitchen to get some supper. After supper was over, Mrs. Rutherford, who made it a rule to question and teach the family every evening, asked any strangers who were present questions, and talked to them about their souls.

When she came to the Archbishop, she said, "Tell me, my good man, how many commandments are there?"

"Oh," said he, "there are *eleven*, madam."

When he said "eleven," Mrs. Rutherford said, "Have you never been taught at school? Has no one ever taught you how many commandments there are?" Then she told him how Moses wrote the ten commandments, and how in the book of Exodus the ten commandments are all written down as simply as possible.

"How is it," said she, "that you know so little?"

Usher hung his head, and said nothing for a time. But when she had finished her questioning, he said very quietly, "There is a word in the Gospel, which says, 'A new commandment give I unto you, That ye love one another;' and I think that a commandment given by our Lord Jesus should be attended to as well as Moses' commandments, and one added to ten makes eleven." They soon discovered it was the great Archbishop Usher, and you can imagine how Mrs. Rutherford felt when she found it out!

Now, my dear children, I hope you will never forget the new commandment given by our Lord Jesus Christ. You are to show a loving spirit. You are to be willing to give up your own way, to be good-natured, to keep your temper. This is love. This is practical Christianity. This is showing that you love Jesus at home. This shows that when you go and ask for help to teach the commandments of God to poor children, you yourselves are trying to keep them.

Try, last of all, to honour all God's commandments in spirit as well as in letter.

There was a place in London where they sold all sorts of things. It was called "The Soho Bazaar." A lady one day took one of her children there, a little girl. The little girl was so pleased with what she saw, that she was tempted to do what she shouldn't. She fell into temptation. I am afraid she did not really *pray* when she said her prayers in the morning.

Well, when she got into the bazaar, she saw some things which looked so very nice that she coveted them. So by and by, as she passed one of the stalls, when her mother was occupied, and she thought no one could see, she picked up a toy, and put it into her pocket. But oh, how heavy that pocket felt! Her conscience began to speak to her! How miserable she felt. Oh, that she had not taken that toy!

As they were coming back, her mother stopped to talk to the woman who kept the same stall, and the poor little girl pulled the toy out of her pocket and put it back without anybody seeing. She went home, and at night she said her prayers. She seemed unhappy. She was thinking of what she had done at the bazaar.

Her mother said, "My dear child, what is the matter ? Do tell me." And as her mother spoke to her in a kind, loving way, her heart was melted, and she said, "Oh, mother, I have been so miserable today. I have not broken a commandment quite. But oh, mother, I have *cracked* a commandment," and then she told her mother everything.

Oh, dear children, take care that you don't *crack* any of the commandments! The *new* commandment I have told you of is in

John chapter 13 verse 34: "Love one another." Remember that. If you wish to help in God's work, do not forget the new commandment : "Love one another." Every one of you can understand that.

The Bible says, "Even a child may be known by his doings." We can soon tell when a little child is trying to keep Christ's new commandment. Keep it whole: don't let it be *cracked* or *scratched*. May God help us all to keep it, with a new heart and a lively faith in Christ! Then when we stand at Christ's judgment-seat, He will say, "Well done, good and faithful servants, enter ye into the joy of your Lord."

Seeking the Lord Early

"I love them that love Me; and those that seek Me early shall find Me."

PROVERBS 8. 17.

Dear Children,

I am going to talk to you about Jesus Christ and your souls.

I want to make you happy. But I know that people are never really happy unless their *souls* are happy; and I am sure that people's souls cannot be happy, unless they love Jesus Christ. And that is the reason why I am going to preach to you now: I want to tell you something about Jesus Christ and your souls.

Dear children, I hope you will listen while I talk to you. I pray that the Spirit of God may come into your hearts, and make you able to do so. Try to listen to me; try to understand what I say; try to remember and carry away something in your minds. I wish to do you all a great deal of good. Do not forget I am speaking to you, not to the grown up people, but to you, only to you.

Now just think what a pleasant text we have got here: it is said, "I love them that love Me; and those that seek Me early shall find Me."

These are sweet words indeed; and who do you think says them? They are said by the Lord Jesus Christ, and Son of God, the Saviour of the world. He is called "Wisdom" in this chapter. But we know it means Jesus Christ, for there are things said about Wisdom in this chapter which cannot be said truly about any one but Jesus Christ Himself.

Come, now, and let us see what Jesus Christ says; listen, dear children, for this is very important.

(1) He tells us, "I love them that love Me." Now what can we make out of this?

First of all, do you not think it is very pleasant to hear that there are people whom Jesus Christ *loves*? You know we all like to be loved in this world: only think how sad it would be for you and me if there was nobody alive who loved us. Suppose that no man or woman cared for us suppose that everybody neglected us, and left us alone. What would we do? We would be wretched, and miserable, and unhappy! I am sure we all like to be loved.

Well, then, just consider what a blessed thing it must be to be loved by Jesus Christ, by the Son of God Himself.

You know that sometimes people love us in this world, and yet can do nothing for us. Your dear fathers and mothers love you, but perhaps they are poor, and cannot buy what you want ; or perhaps they are sick or old and can do very little to help you.

But, dear children, these are things that can never happen to Jesus Christ, and I will tell you why.

Jesus Christ *is very great* : He is King of kings, and Lord of lords. He is Maker of all things. He is God Himself. He is Almighty. He is able to do anything whatsoever He likes.

Oh, what a thing it must be to be loved by Jesus Christ!

And again, Jesus Christ is *very rich*: He has got everything to give you which you could want, either for soul or body. He keeps the keys of heaven. He has got an endless store of blessings in His treasure house, far more than I could describe.

Oh, what a thing it must be to be loved by Jesus Christ!

And again, Jesus Christ is *very good*: In his lifetime, He never refused anyone who asked Him favours in a proper way. He was never known to say, "No!" to any person who made a prayer to Him with a meek and humble heart and today He still hears and answers our prayers in the way that He knows is best.

Oh, what a thing it must be to be loved by Jesus Christ!

Dear children, consider these things:-

Do you want a *great* friend?

Do you want a *rich* friend?

Do you want a *kind* friend?

Is this the sort of friend you would like?

Then be sure there is no friend in all the world like Jesus Christ. There is no love so well worth having as the love of Jesus Christ.

Blessed and happy are those whom Jesus Christ loves. I could not tell you even a tenth of all the great things he does for their souls.

He *pardons all their sins*. He forgives all the bad things they do. He washes them in His own blood, and makes them whiter than snow, so that not a spot remains. Dear children, I think that is just what you and I want. We have all sinned many, many sins.

Also, He *gives them power to become good*. He puts His Spirit in their hearts, and makes them love God's ways and enjoy walking in them. Dear children, that, too, is just the thing you and I want. We have very bad, wicked hearts, by nature. We never love God's ways on our own.

Besides this, *He takes care that none whom He loves shall be lost.* He keeps them as a shepherd keeps his sheep. He will not allow either wicked men or the devil to destroy their souls. Dear children, that, too, is just what you and I want. We are all very weak, foolish creatures ; we should never be safe if left to ourselves.

And lastly, *He is getting ready a place in heaven for those whom He loves.* He has a glorious house for them there, far away from sin, sorrow and trouble. Dear children, that, too, is good news for you and me. Is it not pleasant to think He has prepared a home for us, so that whenever we leave this world we shall go to a place of peace and rest?

All these things the Lord Jesus Christ does for those whom He loves. Look at them! What mighty things, what glorious things they are! He cleanses them from all their sins. He gives them power to be good. He takes care they are not lost. He gets ready a house for them in heaven.

Dear children, this is love indeed ; this is love worth having. Did I not tell you truly, there is nothing in all the world to be compared to Christ's love, there is nothing like being loved by Jesus Christ?

(2) But let us see next who are those that Jesus Christ loves. He tells us in our text. He says,"I love those that love Me."

Now, how shall we know whether we love Jesus Christ or not? This is indeed an important question. Are there no marks or signs, perhaps you will say, by which those who love Him may be found out? Yes, dear children, I think there are ; and what those marks and signs are, I shall now try to show you.

Remember, then, for one thing, *those who love Jesus Christ, believe whatever He says in the Bible.*

The Bible says we are all sinners, lost, perishing sinners ; full of wickedness and deceit ; deserving nothing but God's anger. Many people cannot quite believe this. They cannot bring themselves to think they are so bad. They dislike to be told about it. Not so those who love Jesus Christ , they believe it all. They are ready to say, "It is true, true, quite true."

Again, the Bible tells us we must come to Christ, and trust only in Him, if we want to be saved. It says that nothing but His blood can wash away our sins ; that it is only for His sake that anyone can be forgiven. Many people will not believe this either. They cannot think their own goodness will not help to get them to heaven. But those who love Jesus Christ believe it all. They take the Lord at His word ; they leave off trusting in their own goodness, and are ready to say, "None but Christ, none but Christ is my hope."

Dear children, no-one can love Jesus

Christ who does not believe what He says. Think what a sad thing it would be if you and I could not get our relations to believe us. Think about how hard and unkind it would seem if they were to say, "We do not depend at all on what you tell us, we cannot trust your word." I am sure we would think that they no longer loved us. This, then, is one mark of those who love Jesus Christ, they never doubt what He tells them, they believe every word.

Remember, for another thing, *those who love Jesus Christ try to please Him.* You know when you love people in this world, you try to please them. You try to do what they ask you to do, to behave as they wish you to behave, to remember what they teach you and to listen to what they tell you, and why do you do so ? Because you love them.

And besides this, you try to please them, not only before their faces, when they can see you, but also when they are gone away, and out of sight. True love makes you always think, "What would my dear friends like me to do?"

If your father and mother found you doing naughty things, doing what they told you not to do, they may well say, "Dear child, do you really love me?" Yes, indeed they might. True love will always bring true obedience, and the Bible says, "Even a child is known by his doings." (Prov. 20. 11)

Now, dear children, just as you try to please your friends, if you love them, so do those who love Jesus Christ try to please Him. They are always trying to do His will, to keep His laws, to live by His commandments, to obey His precepts. They do not think that any of Christ's commands are severe; they never say that His laws are hard, strict, and disagreeable. It is their delight to walk in His paths.

Dear children, no man, or woman, or child, can really love Jesus Christ, if they do not try to obey Him. "Ye are my friends," He says, "if ye do whatsoever I command you."

This, then, is another sure mark of those who love Jesus Christ, they try in all things to please Him.

Now we have got through one part of our text. Sit still and think for a moment about what you have heard. Each of you ask your own heart this little question, "Do I love Jesus Christ or not? Do I believe what He says, and do I try to please Him?"

Those who can answer, "Yes," are the children He especially loves. Oh, remember what He says : "I love those that love Me."

(3) But let us look next to the other part of our text, and see what we may learn from it. I really think this part is almost as pleasant as the first, for it contains a sweet promise : "Those that seek Me early shall find Me."

Dear children, how are you and I to seek Jesus Christ? He does not live upon earth like one of us ; we cannot see Him with our eyes ; we cannot reach Him and take hold of Him with our hands ; and yet He says, "Those that seek Me shall find Me." What can this mean ? Let me try to tell you.

First of all, *you must seek Jesus Christ in His own book.*

The Bible is Jesus Christ's book, and all who want to know Him must read their Bibles. He says to everyone of you, "Search the Scriptures," and He will give the Holy Spirit to those who seek Him in the Scriptures, and teach them all about Himself.

Dear children, be regular readers of the Bible all your lives. Let the word dwell in you richly, and then you will be truly wise. Read it daily, read a great deal of it, try and remember it, learn texts by heart.

I remember a little girl in my first parish, who could learn seventy verses of the Bible in a week. How pleasant it is to find the Apostle Paul reminding Timothy, that from a child he had known the Holy Scriptures. Now, why should not all of you be like Timothy in this? I should like to hear that you were all Bible-reading children. Children who read the Bible at home as well as at church.

This, then, is one way to seek Jesus Christ. You must seek Him in the Bible.

Secondly: *you must seek Jesus Christ in His own house.*

Jesus Christ has many houses in this country, where people meet together to pray to Him, and to hear about Him. This Church is one of them; and wherever two or three are gathered together in Jesus Christ's name, the Lord Himself is really present, though we cannot see Him with our eyes.

Dear children, I hope you will all regularly go to Jesus Christ's house as long as you live. I hope you will never do like those foolish people who keep away from it. Oh, what sad harm they are doing to their poor souls!

And when you go, try to listen to

all you hear, and to get good from it. Do not look about, and make a noise, or talk to other children, but listen well to all that is read or preached. Jesus Christ is there, and sees how you behave. He loves to see little children coming to His house, and behaving well; and if you persevere in so doing, you may be sure He will put His Spirit in you, and fill you with all knowledge.

This, then, is another way to seek Jesus Christ. You must seek Him in His house.

Thirdly : *you must seek Jesus Christ on your knees in prayer.*

You must ask Him with your own mouth to give you everything that your soul wants. You must ask Him to cleanse you from all your sins in His blood. To give you His Spirit. To make you good, obedient, gentle, kind and truth-speaking children. To keep you from being selfish, idle, greedy, angry, cunning, or bad-tempered. You must tell Him all you are afraid of, and all you feel, and all you wish to have for your soul. This is prayer.

You need not be afraid of Him at all when you pray. He would like you to tell Him everything in your own simple way, just as you tell your own mothers when you want anything. He loves children very much. He was once displeased with His disciples, because they prevented people bringing their children to Him, and He said, "Suffer the little children to come unto Me, and forbid them not." And He is just the same now that He was then.

Dear children, I should like you all to be praying children. Children who tell the Lord all your needs, and are not afraid to speak to Him. Prayer is the surest way to seek Him, and without prayer your souls will never prosper.

Never mind if your prayers seem very poor and weak. Only let them come from your hearts, and the Lord hears them.

The Lord Jesus hears every prayer

that is prayed to Him in earnest. The least prayer of a little child on earth is loud enough to be heard clearly in heaven above. Heaven seems to be a long way off, but you may be sure the very moment the prayer is spoken it is heard there. A little key will often open a great door. Prayer is a little key of that sort. It can open the door of heaven, and take you up to the very throne of God Himself. Blessed are they who delight in prayer, and call much upon God.

This, then, is the third way to seek the Lord Jesus Christ. You must seek Him in prayer.

Dear children, I have told you how to seek the Lord. Ask yourselves, each one of you, before you go any further : Do I really seek Him?

(4) But our text tells us something about those who seek Jesus Christ, and what is it? It says they "shall find Him."

The Lord promises "they that seek Me shall find Me." How sweet it is to hear that. Think how disappointing it would be to seek and seek all our lives, and have our trouble for nothing, and never find Him. But the Lord says, *"they shall find Me."*

Now I want to tell you what this "finding" means. We shall not see Him with our eyes, for He is sitting at God's right hand in heaven, and not on earth, and yet we are told we shall find Him. How can this be? Let me tell you.

You will find the Lord's presence in your own hearts and minds. You will feel something within you, as if the Lord Jesus Christ was sitting by you, taking care of you, putting His arm round you, smiling upon you and speaking kindly to you. Just as a blind person feels brighter and happier when the sun is shining pleasantly on him, though he cannot see it, so you and I, if we seek Jesus Christ in earnest, shall soon feel our hearts lighter and happier. Something within us will tell us that we have found Him.

Dear children, it is sweet and comfortable indeed when we feel that we have really found Jesus Christ. Oh, that you may never give up seeking till you have found Him and I know that you will find Him if you keep seeking, for He is not far off. He is very near every one of us, He is waiting for us to call upon Him.

When you have found Him, you will feel as if you had got a sure Friend in whom you can trust. A Friend who will always love you, always watch over you, always take care of you, always be good to you, never fail you.

When you have found Him, you will feel as if you have got strength and power to walk in God's ways; strength to keep yourself from bad words and bad company; strength to do things which please God.

When you have found Him, you will feel as if you had got a pleasant Comforter living in your heart. You will be far more happy, and cheerful, and content, than you were before. Little things will not put you out as they used to do. You will not be afraid of sickness, or pain, or death.

Dear children, how delightful it will be to feel all this. Try, all of you, do try to find Jesus Christ.

(5) And now there is only one thing more in our text that I want to talk to you about. Only one little word. But that little word is so very important, that I dare not pass over it. It is the word *"early."* "They that seek Me early," the Lord Jesus Christ says, "they are those that shall find Me."

Dear children, that word *"early"* was meant particularly for yourselves. Seeking Jesus Christ early means seeking Jesus Christ when you are quite young, and that is just what I want you all to do.

Children, the Lord sends a message to you all this very day by my mouth. He says He should like you to begin seeking Him at once.

Now, do remember, all of you, you cannot begin seeking Jesus too soon.

Seeking early is the *safest* way. Children may be young and healthy; but no children are too young and healthy to die. For death is very strong: it can soon make the healthiest of you weaken away, and make your rosy cheeks pale and sickly. And death is very cruel: it does not mind whom he takes away out of families, and it will not wait for anyone to get ready; it will take you just when it pleases.

I think just as many young persons die as old ones. I see the names of just as many young people as old on the grave stones. Children, you would not like to die without having sought the Lord at all. Oh, remember, seeking early is the safest way.

And then, besides this, seeking early is the *happiest way*. Surely, if it is so pleasant to have Jesus Christ for a friend, the sooner you have Him for a friend the better. You cannot think how happy a child's life goes on when his ways please the Lord. Everything seems bright and cheerful; lessons seem more easy, and play seems more pleasant; friends seem more kind, and trouble seems less troublesome; and everything in life seems more smooth. Dear children, I want you to enjoy all this. Then make haste and do not delay to seek the Lord.

And last of all, seeking early is the *easiest way*. When you and I have got a great deal of work to do, you know there is nothing like beginning in good time. Now this is just what you should do about your souls; you should begin in good time to seek Him who alone can save them. People that have got work to do that must be finished before dark, take care to get up early in the morning. So should you do, dear children, in working about your souls. You should seek the Lord in the morning of life, and get your work done before the night of death cometh, when no-one can work. Every year you put it off you will find it harder work , more to be done, and less time to do it. Every year you will find your hearts more stubborn, more unwilling to do what is right.

Now your hearts are like young trees, so soft and tender, that by the Lord's help you may bend them any way. In a few years they will be like strong thick trees, so tough and well rooted, that nothing but a mighty wind can shake them. Dear children, begin to seek the Lord at once. I want you to have as few difficulties as possible in your journey to heaven.

Consider these things, consider these things well, and begin early to seek the Lord. It is the *safest* way, the *happiest* way, the *easiest* way.

Try to be like Obadiah, who feared the Lord from his youth. Try to be like our blessed Lord Jesus Christ Himself, who grew up "in favour with God and man."

Think of the day when Jesus Christ shall come again to this world. He will come again in the clouds of heaven, with power and great glory. He will come very suddenly, in an hour when no man expects it; like a thief in the night. He will gather together all who love Him, and take them home to His Father's house, to be for ever happy. He will leave behind all the idle, and wicked, and unbelieving persons, who have not sought Him, to be wretched and miserable for ever.

Dear children, Jesus Christ might come very soon. We do not know how soon. How sad it would then be to see others taken up to heaven, and ourselves left behind! How dreadful to feel, "I might have been taken up too, but I would not seek the Lord!"

Think, too, of the great day of judgment; when all of us shall stand before God, and have to give account of our works. Some of the people who are saved, will say then, "I never began to seek Jesus Christ till I was forty years old, and I wasted away more than half my life." Others will say, "I never began to seek Him till I was twenty, and I wasted many years of my life."

But some will be able to say, "I sought the Lord when I was quite young and I can hardly remember the time when I did not try to love Him."

Dear children, how pleasant it will be for those people to think this! How sweet to feel that they gave the first days of their lives as well as the last to Jesus Christ! How glorious they will appear who have loved their Saviour in the beginning of their time, as well as in the end. The Lord grant that many of you may be found among them. Oh, seek the Lord early! Seek Him while He may be found.

And now, dear children, it is time for me to leave off and let you go.

Perhaps I shall never see you all together again in this world ; indeed, I am almost sure I shall not. But we shall

all meet at the last day. I do hope you will think of what I have told you about Jesus Christ and your souls.

Remember, I want you all to be happy children, and in order to be happy you must love Jesus Christ.

THE END.